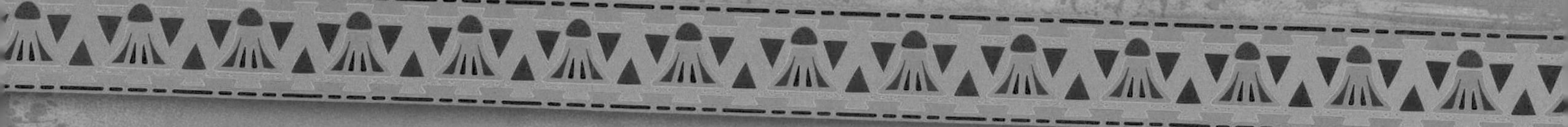

First published in Great Britain in 2017 by Wayland

ISBN 978 1 5263 0086 7
10 9 8 7 6 5 4 3 2 1

Wayland
An imprint of Hachette Children's Group
Part of Hodder & Stoughton
Carmelite House
50 Victoria Embankment
London EC4Y 0DZ

An Hachette UK Company
www.hachette.co.uk
www.hachettechildrens.co.uk

A catalogue record for this title is available from the British Library

Printed and bound in China

Produced for Wayland by
White-Thomson Publishing Ltd
www.wtpub.co.uk

Editor: Claudia Martin
Designer: Clare Nicholas
Picture researcher: Claudia Martin
Illustrations: Julian Baker
Wayland editor: Vicky Brooker
Consultant: Philip Parker

Picture acknowledgements:
The author and publisher would like to thank the following agencies and people for allowing these pictures to be reproduced:

Alamy/Anders Blomqvist 15 (bottom); Alamy/Collection Dagli Orti/The Art Archive 15 (top), 18 (left) and 20; Alamy/Robert Harding 13 (top) and 23 (bottom); Alamy/Angelo Hornak 5 (bottom); Alamy/Christopher Klein/National Geographic Creative 15 (bottom); Alamy/World History Archive 12 (bottom); Julian Baker 18 (right) and 19; Stefan Chabluk 4 and 8; Dreamstime/Shaikhkamalk1 front cover (bottom); Mary Evans/Iberfoto front cover (centre right); Bernard Gagnon 9 (bottom); Usman Ghani 6; Ismoon/Chhatrapati Shivaji Maharaj Vastu Sangrahalaya 21 (top); Ismoon/National Museum, New Delhi 1 (right), 23 (top), 28 (left); National Museum, New Delhi 24 and 32; Photo Researchers/Mary Evans front cover (top left and right); Saqib Qayyum 7 (bottom); Royroydeb/Indian Museum, Kolkata 29 (top); Shutterstock/AJP 10; Shutterstock/Asianet-Pakistan 26; Shutterstock/Marijus Auruskevicius 17 (bottom); Shutterstock/Aztec Images 16; Shutterstock/Cornfield 11 (top); Shutterstock/Hippiekoala 27 (top); Shutterstock/Jacek Kadaj 11 (bottom); Shutterstock/Maradon333 12 (top); Shutterstock/Vladimir Melnik 1 (left) and 28 (bottom); Shutterstock/Shyamala Muralinath 17 (top); Shutterstock/Maks Narodenko: 3; Shutterstock/Vadim Petrakov 5 (top); Shutterstock/Ann Taylor 9 (top); Shutterstock/Travel Stock 25 (top) and 31; Siyajkak 21 (bottom); Smn121 28 (top right); Soban 13 (bottom), 14, 22 and 29 (bottom); Obed Suhail 7 (top); Wellcome Images 27 (bottom).

All design elements from Shutterstock.

Contents

Who lived in the Indus Valley?

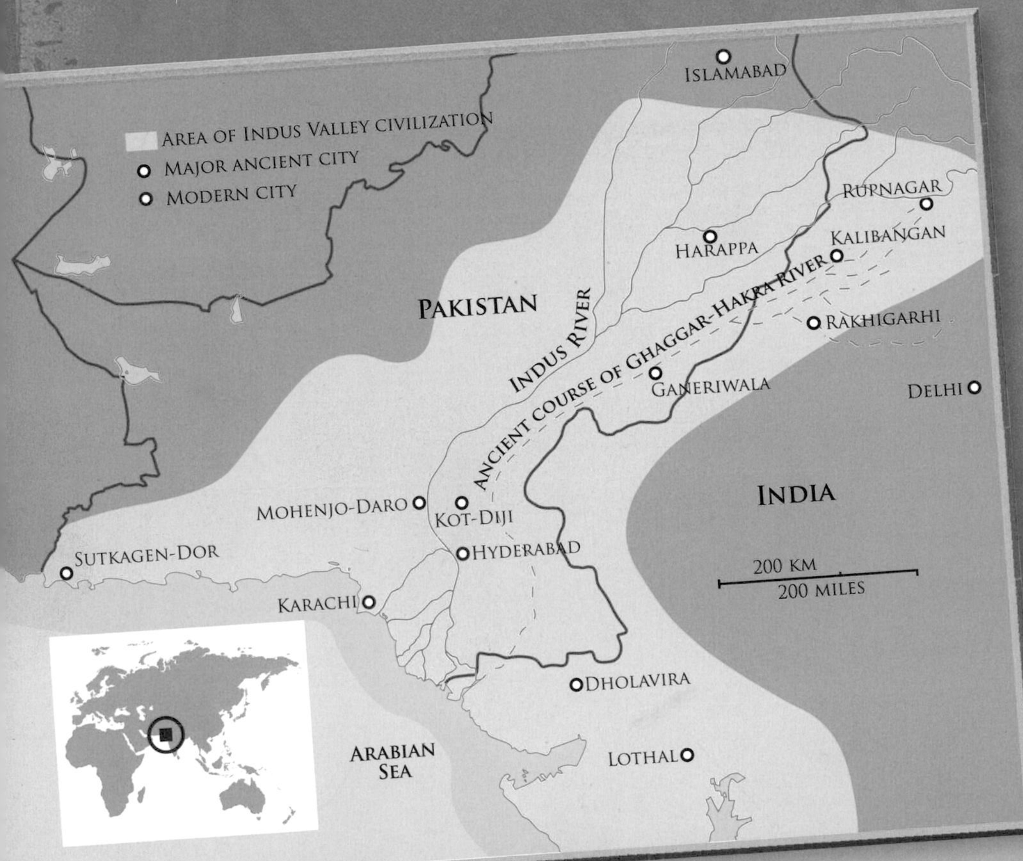

Around 4,000 years ago, the Indus Valley, in present-day Pakistan and India, was home to a great civilisation. The people who lived there were farmers, craftspeople, traders and leaders.

Between 2600 BCE and 1900 BCE, about 5 million people lived in the cities and villages of the Indus Valley. These were some of the earliest cities in the world.

First cities

The first people in the Indus Valley were hunters. They tracked wild animals and searched for plants to eat. But about 8,000 years ago, Indus Valley people learned to farm. As their skills got better over the centuries, they were able to grow enough food not only to feed their families, but extra to sell. Some people could leave farming to become potters or weavers. Others became traders, selling what craftspeople made. By 2600 BCE, cities had grown up around markets.

Today, the Indus River still brings life to the dried-out land.

Rivers of life

The Indus Valley civilisation grew up around the Indus and Ghaggar-Hakra Rivers. This region is hot and dry, apart from during the monsoon season. The rivers gave people almost everything they needed to live: water for their crops and for drinking, cooking and washing, as well as fish to eat. Boats loaded with food and goods travelled up and down the rivers.

How do we know?

Eventually, the Indus Valley cities fell into ruin and were buried by earth, but some have been excavated by archaeologists. Among the buildings, they have found artefacts, such as tools, jewellery and statues, that tell us about Indus Valley life. Scientists have examined skeletons found in graves, and ancient food in rubbish pits.

Archaeologists study artefacts such as this carving of a squirrel eating a nut, which was made by an Indus Valley craftsperson over 4,000 years ago.

Great cities

There were dozens of cities in the Indus Valley, and thousands of towns and villages. The largest cities were carefully planned and cleverly constructed.

Biggest city

The biggest city was Mohenjo-Daro, which was home to about 40,000 people. It was split into two parts. On a brick platform, above the reach of the Indus River's floods, was the walled Citadel. Archaeologists have found the ruins of large and important-looking buildings here. These may have been temples or government buildings. In the Lower City were homes, workshops and markets. Different trades, such as metalworking or pottery, were in separate areas.

Mohenjo-Daro was abandoned in around 1800 BCE. Its buildings collapsed and were covered by earth, until they were excavated by archaeologists in the 1920s.

Sewers

The cities of the Indus Valley were the first in the world to have sewer systems. Human waste and dirty water were flushed away from homes along clay pipes. These drains fed into wider sewers that ran beneath main streets, carrying the waste downhill and out of the city. Fresh water was collected from public brick-lined wells. Many houses also had their own private wells.

In these public baths in the city of Harappa, people scooped water from the well with a jar, then stood on brick-paved platforms to wash themselves.

The Great Bath

In Mohenjo-Daro's Citadel, archaeologists have named one building the Great Bath. It contains a structure that looks very much like a modern swimming pool. Some people think it was a public bath. Others think the pool's central location suggests it was used for important religious ceremonies.

The Great Bath is 12 m (39 ft) long and 7 m (22 ft) wide. It was made watertight by bitumen tar, spread between two layers of bricks.

At home

Poorer families lived in small, simple homes. In the summer, they slept on the roof to keep cool. Richer families lived in grander homes with several rooms.

Cool courtyards

Most homes were built around an open-air courtyard. Here families could work and play in the shade. Some homes had an upper storey for sleeping in, with balconies over the courtyard. To protect houses from noise and dust, the windows and doors opened onto the courtyard and side alleys rather than the main street. Many houses had what looks like a rubbish bin on their outer wall.

STAIRS
KITCHEN
COURTYARD
BATH ROOM
ENTRANCE

This plan of a large Indus Valley home shows cooking and living areas opening off the central courtyard. Stairs lead to an upper floor.

Mud bricks are still made in Pakistan and India today, using clay and soil mixed with water, then pressed into wooden moulds.

Mud bricks

There is little stone available in the Indus Valley, so homes and other buildings were constructed from bricks made from clay and mud. Lower walls, sewers and wells needed to be sturdy, so these were made from mud bricks that had been baked at high temperatures in a kiln. Upper walls were built from mud bricks dried in the sun, as these lighter bricks kept the living areas cool.

Flushing toilets

Cleanliness and hygiene seem to have been very important to Indus Valley people. Most homes, even small ones, had a separate bathroom. Here people washed and went to the toilet, then flushed waste down the drain with a jar of water. At this time, most other people in the world would have been quite dirty, and human sewage was a major cause of disease.

In the city of Lothal, houses had a bathroom with a brick-tiled washing area. Toilets had a brick seat.

Farming and food

Historians think that Indus Valley people had diets rather like people in the region today. They ate grains, meat and fish, kept fresher and made tasty by spices.

Working the fields

Farmers planted their fields twice a year, so there was always fresh food. In winter, important crops were the grains wheat and barley, along with peas, lentils and mustard greens. In summer, it was the turn of millet, sesame for oil, and cotton for cloth. Fields were close to the river as irrigation canals or buckets could carry water only a short distance. Fruit trees offered apricots, dates, figs and mangoes.

Bulls or other cattle pulled ploughs through the fields, turning up new soil ready for seeds.

Like this Indian fisherman today, ancient people used nets, as well as hooks, to catch river fish.

Fish and meat

Indus Valley people ate lots of fish, from the sea as well as the nearby rivers. After fishermen landed their catch from the Arabian Sea, the fish were preserved by drying or salting, then carried hundreds of kilometres inland. Farmers also kept herds of cows, buffalo, sheep and goats for meat, milk and yoghurt.

Mealtimes

Food was cooked at the hearth, in pottery and metal frying pans and pots. Grains such as wheat, barley and millet were ground on a stone and made into bread and porridge, which might have been sweetened with honey. Meat, fish and lentil dishes were spiced with ginger, turmeric, cinnamon and garlic.

Bread was probably made by the same methods as today. The dough is kneaded then baked on a hot stone over the fire or in an oven.

Rulers of the valley

We have not found any palaces, or monuments that celebrate great rulers, so historians are not sure who ruled the Indus Valley.

Laying down the law

Although we have not found evidence of kings and queens, we know the Indus Valley was an organised place. Someone, perhaps a group of people, set down rules about how things should be done. For example, all bricks were exactly the same size and shape. Someone oversaw the construction of sewer systems and employed people to unblock the drains.

The same units of weight were used by everyone, to make sure trade was fair. Scales – and weights like these – measured out grain or beads.

The priest-king

In 1927, an interesting statue was found in Mohenjo-Daro. It is carefully carved from stone and is 17.5 cm (7 in) tall. It shows a man wearing a jewelled headband and armband, and a cloak patterned with trefoils. In other ancient civilisations, these three-leafed shapes were linked with the gods and stars. Perhaps the statue is of a priest, or a priest-king.

The priest-king statue tells us a little about how people looked. The man has a neatly trimmed beard and a shaved upper lip.

A peaceful place?

Very few weapons have been found in Indus Valley cities, which suggests they were largely peaceful. But all the cities were surrounded by strong, high walls, so attacks must have been feared. We can guess there were long periods of peace from the orderly way the cities were constructed. They were built on a grid plan, in square blocks.

In Mohenjo-Daro's Lower Town, blocks were divided by narrow lanes. All the city streets were straight and ran either east-west or north-south.

Arts and crafts

This model of a trader's cart pulled by two bullocks was made by a potter more than 4,000 years ago.

Many city-dwellers were craftspeople. They made beautiful objects from metal, clay, stone and precious gems. Some of these objects have survived to this day.

Heaps of pottery

Working with clay, which was later baked in a kiln, potters made everyday objects like cooking pots, storage jars and serving platters. They also made countless figurines of people and animals, from birds to bulls. Some figurines were probably toys for children. Perhaps others were of gods and goddesses and were placed in household shrines, where they were used for worship.

Precious jewellery

Both men and women wore jewellery. Men wore necklaces and bangles, while women also wore earrings, brooches, rings, hair ornaments and elaborate belts. These were wrought from metals such as gold, silver, copper and bronze. Beads, carved from ivory, shell, agate and carnelian, decorated necklaces and belts.

This necklace belonged to a wealthy person. It is made from gold, the precious stone jade, and the minerals agate and jasper.

Trading near and far

Money was not used in the Indus Valley. Goods were swapped for other goods of equal value. Raw materials were brought to the cities by rowing boats, on bullock carts, and in bags on the backs of sheep and goats. Jade came from Central Asia, to the north; amethyst gemstones came from the southeast, in present-day India. Finished products were carried to customers as far away as Mesopotamia, in present-day Iraq.

This modern illustration shows bead traders measuring out beads using scales and stone weights. They are studying the quality of gemstones.

A day in the life

In around 5000 BCE, people in the Indus Valley started to make pots and jars by pinching and coiling clay. From 3750 BCE, potters used a new invention: the potter's wheel. This fictional diary entry describes the life of a potter in Mohenjo-Daro.

Shaping a jar on a potter's wheel

My oldest daughter wakes me early. In the courtyard, my wife has laid out a breakfast of porridge, apricots and dates. My two oldest sons, aged seven and ten, eat with me. The boys will spend the day working beside me.

After we have eaten, the boys and I walk to the public baths to bathe and chat with friends. In this corner of the city, we are all potters. When we get home, my wife and older daughter are singing as they weave cloth. My littlest daughter, aged five, is playing noisily with the dog.

My potter's wheel is a circular wooden board, attached by an axle to a flywheel set in a pit in the courtyard. My youngest son turns the flywheel with his foot. I throw a lump of clay on the board, to make a jar for oil. I press my thumb in the centre to hollow it, moulding with my fingers to form the jar's shape. I will make 30 jars today. My oldest son is decorating dried pots with a leaf pattern, using a brush dipped in red paint made from the mineral ochre.

A jar ready for drying

After lunch, we stack the kiln with painted pots. The bottom of the kiln has holes in it, and there is a chimney at the top for releasing smoke. The kiln rests above a pit, where we light a fire of dried cow dung. I ask the gods to protect my house from being set alight. By sunset, these pots will be fired.

Jars placed in a kiln for firing

The diary entry on these pages has been written for this book. Can you create your own diary entry for another person who lived in an Indus Valley city? It could be a bead trader or a priest. Use the facts in this book and in other sources to help you write about a day in their life.

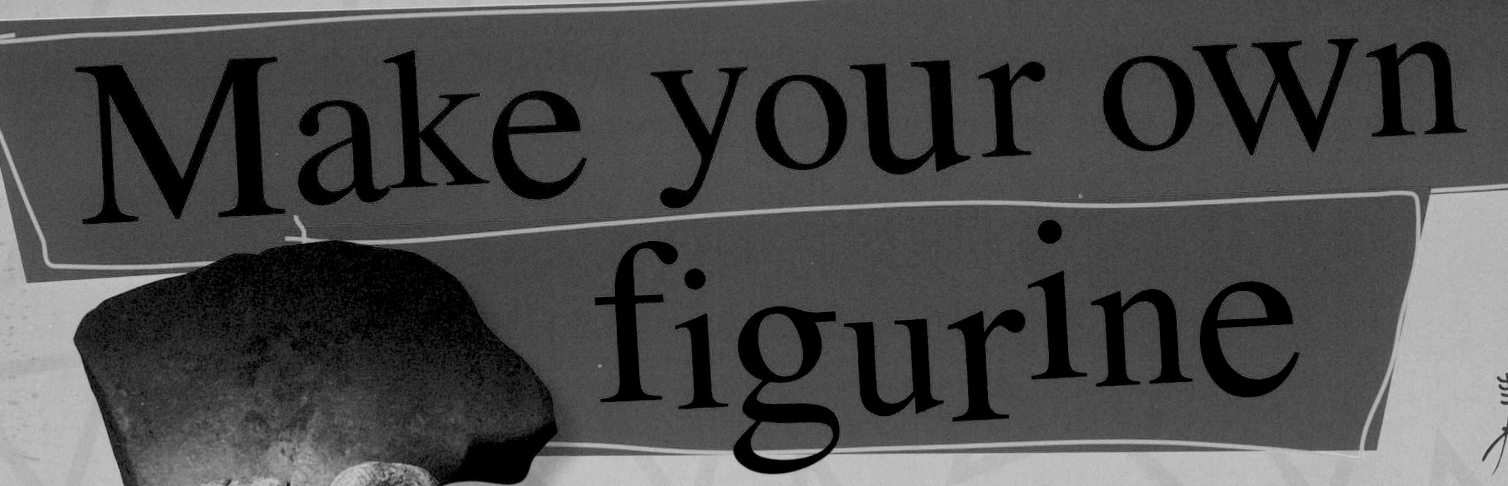

Make your own figurine

Hundreds of clay figurines of people have been found in the Indus Valley. Many historians think they were used for worshipping the gods. Make your own figurine of a woman, perhaps a mother-goddess, using modelling clay.

This figurine was made in Mohenjo-Daro between 2500 and 2000 BCE. It once had legs, which have broken off.

You will need:
- modelling clay or air-drying clay
- ruler and pencil

1 Start by forming the head, body and legs. Indus Valley figurines were 10–30 cm (4–12 in) tall. Roll a thick sausage, then gently squeeze it to make a neck. Press a line between the two legs with a ruler or pencil.

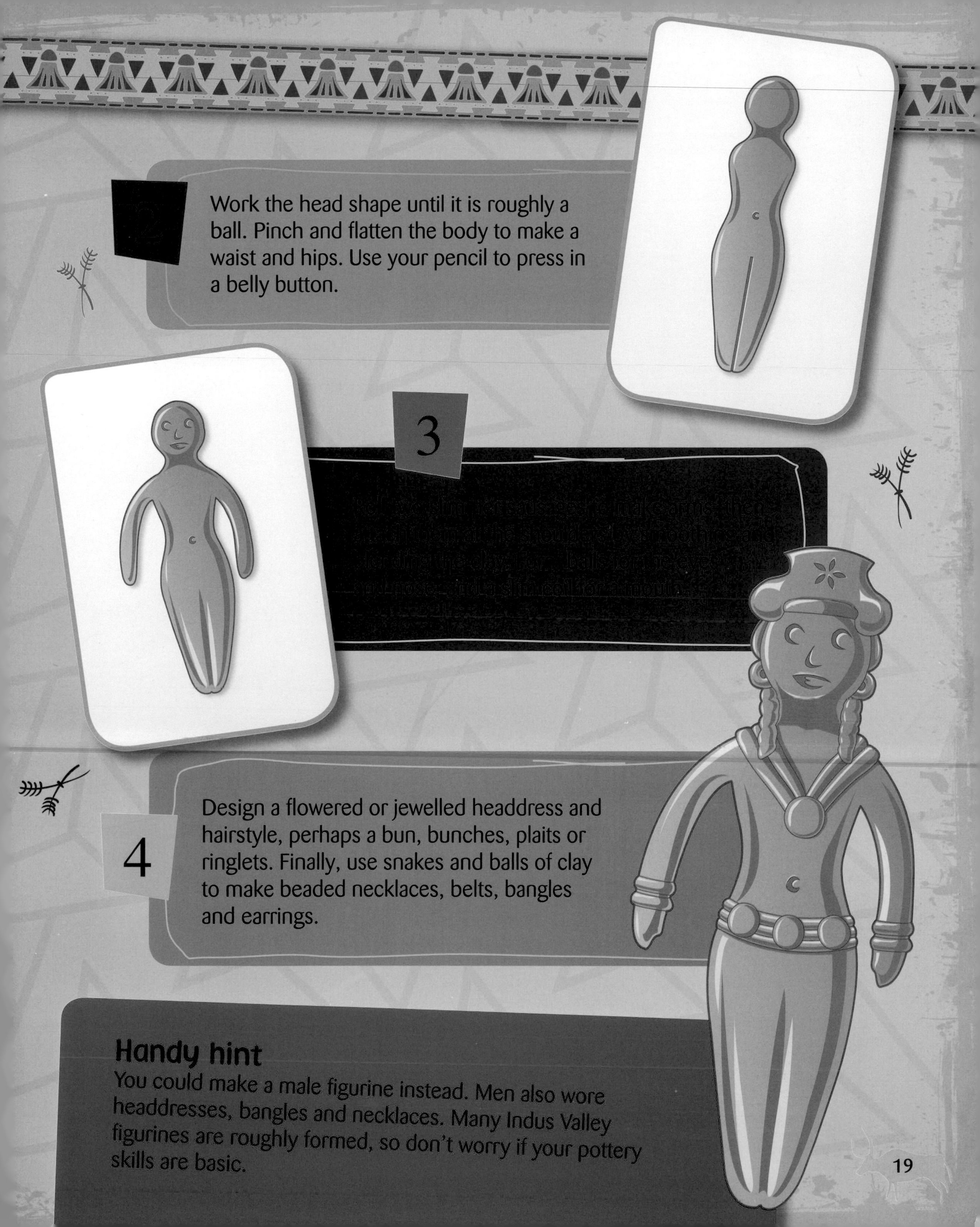

Work the head shape until it is roughly a ball. Pinch and flatten the body to make a waist and hips. Use your pencil to press in a belly button.

3

Roll two slim [illegible] sausages to make arms, then attach them at the shoulders by smoothing and blending the clay. Form balls for the eyes and nose and a slim coil for a mouth.

4

Design a flowered or jewelled headdress and hairstyle, perhaps a bun, bunches, plaits or ringlets. Finally, use snakes and balls of clay to make beaded necklaces, belts, bangles and earrings.

Handy hint

You could make a male figurine instead. Men also wore headdresses, bangles and necklaces. Many Indus Valley figurines are roughly formed, so don't worry if your pottery skills are basic.

Writing on seals

Archaeologists have found more than 3,500 stone seals in the Indus Valley. Seals were pressed into soft clay to create tags for goods, probably to show who owned them.

This seal might have belonged to a trader or family whose symbol was a rhinoceros.

Marking goods

Seals were usually carved from soft soapstone then fired in a kiln to harden them. They are about 2.5 cm (1 in) square. On their back is a loop, through which a cord was run for hanging round the neck. Most seals show an animal, above which are symbols.

Unicorns

Many different kinds of local animals are shown on seals, from elephants and tigers to cattle such as bulls, water buffalo and zebu. The most common animal found on seals is the unicorn, a mythical creature that must have been important to Indus Valley people.

This is a mould taken from a unicorn seal, dipped in plaster: the design is reversed so it stands up. When pressed into clay, a seal would have left an imprint like this of its owner's unique design.

Strange writing

The symbols on seals were probably a form of writing. Symbols have also been found on Indus Valley pots and a few other objects. Historians have spotted more than 400 different symbols but cannot work out what they mean because there is nothing to compare them with. We can guess that the writing on seals gave information about the trader or their goods.

 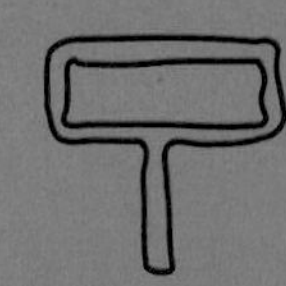      

These symbols were on a sign that hung over the gate to the Citadel of the city of Dholavira. What do you think they mean?

Entertainment

Some of the objects found in the Indus Valley tell us what people did in their spare time. We know that they listened to music, danced and played games.

Toys

Although adults and older children had to work hard, all sorts of toys and games were among the ruins of Indus Valley homes. There were board games that look like chess, as well as some with ivory counters, marbles and dice. Young children played with mini carts, clay rattles, spinning tops, puppets and wheel-along animals with nodding heads.

Clay maze puzzles with balls must have been popular, because they have been found in several Indus Valley cities.

Dancing to music

Metal, stone and clay figurines have been found showing girls in elegant dancing poses. We have also found many whistles in the shape of birds. One seal shows a stringed harp-like instrument. These finds suggest that people enjoyed listening to music and watching dancers, or joining in themselves.

This bronze statue of a dancing girl was made in about 2500 BCE. She is naked apart from her bangles and necklace but she looks self-confident.

Pets

Some families kept dogs and cats as pets. Their skeletons and paw prints have been found among the city streets. Clay birdcages and figurines tell us that Indus Valley people probably kept small songbirds in their homes. Monkeys and peacocks may also have been pets, as they were in other ancient civilisations.

Dog figurines show different breeds, from low and squat to tall like a hound. This one is wearing a collar.

Religion

In this seal, a male figure wearing a horned headdress is seated on a throne, surrounded by wild animals. Could he be a god who holds power over animals?

There are no pictures or understandable writings to tell us exactly what Indus Valley people believed. However, we can make guesses based on what other peoples of the time believed, and on what people in the region believe today.

Gods and goddesses

We cannot know for sure what gods and goddesses were worshipped by Indus Valley people, but many seals and figurines show powerful-looking people who may have been gods. There are many figurines of naked women who may have been mother-goddesses. In other ancient civilisations, mother-goddesses were believed to bring new life to the fields and to families.

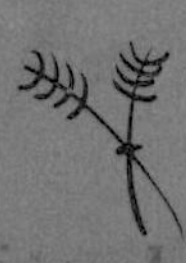

Bathing

Water, bathing and cleanliness were very important to the people of the Indus Valley. One of the largest buildings in Mohenjo-Daro was the Great Bath. Many historians believe that water and bathing were part of the Indus Valley religion. The Indian religion Hinduism may have its roots in the religion of the Indus Valley. Bathing is important to modern Hindus.

Hindus believe that daily bathing rituals are important not just for the health of the body but for the health of the soul.

The dead

Indus Valley people buried their dead. They dressed their bodies in jewellery and filled graves with containers of food and drink. In this way, they hoped to prepare their loved-ones for the afterlife. In the dying days of the Indus Valley civilisation, the objects placed in graves were poorer quality.

This skeleton was unearthed from a 5,000-year-old Indus Valley grave.

Abandoned cities

By around 1700 BCE, the Indus Valley cities had been abandoned. Over time, people forgot how to understand the writing system and even the locations of the cities.

Decay and disaster

From about 1900 BCE, the Indus Valley civilisation was in decline. Craftspeople stopped making their most beautiful work. New buildings were roughly constructed. Trade with other areas died away. Two hundred years later, almost everyone had left the cities. What happened? Most historians think the climate became drier. This made the Ghaggar-Hakra River dry up for most of the year. The Indus River changed its course, causing flooding in some places and lack of water in others.

Flooding is common in the Indus Valley today. This family has had to abandon their home.

Indus Valley people probably took their farming skills with them. Today, Indian farmers grow the same crops as Indus Valley farmers, using similar methods.

Moving on

Although some Indus Valley people died from hunger or disease, many moved eastward, into present-day India. They probably set up home in other river valleys, such as around the Ganges River. There were no cities there at first, but a few hundred years later, around 1200 BCE, powerful cities began to grow.

Remembering the past

Some Indus Valley skills were lost, such as how to build sewer systems. But survivors passed on other skills and beliefs to their children. For example, the many bangles worn by some Hindu women today are similar to those made by Indus Valley craftspeople. Like their ancestors, modern Hindus worship god in the forms of a mother-goddess, Parvati, and a god who controls the beasts, Shiva.

This illustration shows the Hindu gods Shiva and Parvati sitting on a tiger skin. The Ganges River flows from Shiva's head. Can you see any similarities with the seal on page 24?

Facts and figures

The Indus Valley was home to some of the earliest known rulers, for measuring bricks and other materials. They were made from ivory and date from 1800 BCE.

Over 1,000 Indus Valley cities and villages have been found by archaeologists, but only around 100 of them have been excavated.

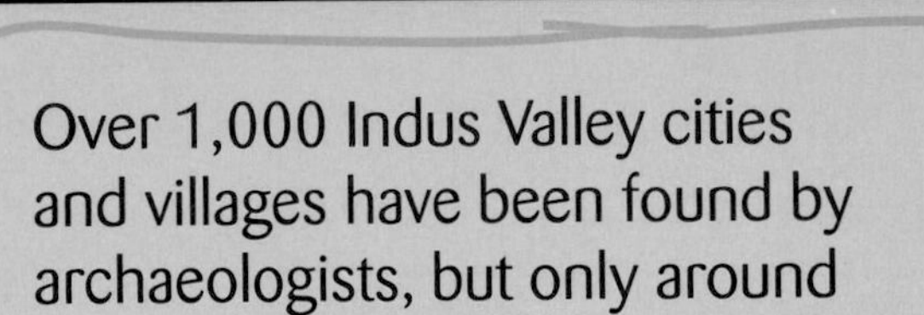

Figurines show us that women wore their hair in elaborate styles, such as plaits, ponytails and ringlets, decorated with flowers and combs.

There were more than 700 wells in the city of Mohenjo-Daro.

Although Indus Valley cities were huge, most of the people in the region lived in villages in the countryside.

By examining the skeletons and teeth of Indus Valley people, experts have discovered they were usually quite healthy. But men were often better fed than women.

Timeline

6500 BCE	Hunters begin to settle down to farming in the Indus Valley.
5000 BCE	Indus Valley people are making pottery.
3300 BCE	Towns are growing up in the region. Craftspeople are making tools from metals such as bronze.
2600 BCE	The major cities, such as Mohenjo-Daro and Harappa, are being planned and constructed.
1900 BCE	The Indus Valley cities are in decline, and many people are moving away.
1700 BCE	The cities are almost completely abandoned.
1853 CE	Archaeologists start to excavate Indus Valley cities.

Glossary

afterlife Life after death.

agate A stone used in jewellery that often shows bands of different colours.

ancestor A person related to you who lived a long time ago.

archaeologist A person who studies history by examining ancient buildings and objects.

artefact An object made by human beings.

BCE The letters 'BCE' stand for 'before the common era'. They are used to signify dates before the birth of Jesus.

CE The letters 'CE' stand for 'common era'. They are used to signify dates since the birth of Jesus.

ceremony A public event, often linked with religion or an important date.

citadel A strong castle or fortress, in or near a city.

craftsperson A person who is skilled at making things by hand.

decline A slow loss of power or importance.

evidence Facts or objects that can prove the truth of something.

excavated Uncovered by digging in the ground carefully.

figurine A small statue.

flywheel A wheel that is turned to move other parts of a machine.

grains The seeds of food plants, such as wheat, rice or oats.

hearth The floor of a fireplace.

Hinduism A religion that grew up in the region of India and Pakistan between 1500 BCE and 300 CE.

hygiene Keeping your body and surroundings clean in order to stay healthy.

irrigation Carrying water to growing crops, using methods such as pipes and ditches.

kiln An oven for baking pottery or bricks.

lapis lazuli A blue rock used in jewellery.

mineral A solid formed naturally in the Earth.

monsoon The rainy season in South Asia.

mythical Existing only in the imagination; talked about in traditional stories.

raw material A basic material, such as wood or clay, that can be used to make something.

ritual A set of actions done in a particular way, often as part of a ceremony.

seal An object with a design carved on it, used to stamp goods or papers.

sewer An underground pipe for carrying waste water and human waste.

shrine A place used for prayer and often to display religious objects.

trader A person who buys and sells goods.

Further reading

Indus Valley (Great Civilizations),
Anita Ganeri (Franklin Watts, 2014)

Indus Valley City (Building History),
Gillian Clements (Franklin Watts, 2008)

The Indus Valley (The History Detective Investigates),
Claudia Martin (Wayland, 2014)

Websites

http://www.ancientindia.co.uk/
Play games, read a diary entry and explore the cities of the Indus Valley on the British Museum's website.

http://www.bbc.co.uk/schools/indusvalley/
Watch videos about Indus Valley life and examine some interesting artefacts.

https://www.harappa.com/
This is an in-depth guide to the Indus Valley and the objects found there, written by historians and archaeologists.

https://www.q-files.com/history/india/ancient-india/
Discover how the Indus Valley civilisation fits into the wider history of the region.